The Best of

Akbar and Birbal

Compiled by Mrs Rungeen Singh

Young Learner Publications ™

G-1, Rattan Jyoti,
18, Rajendra Place
New Delhi-110008 (INDIA)
Ph.: 25750801, 25820556
Fax : 91-11-25764396

Printed at
Thakur Enterprises
Delhi

CONTENTS

A STEP TO DEATH

Akbar was coming down the stairs of the library with Birbal. There were too many steps and Akbar was feeling bored.

Akbar said, "Birbal, do you see these steps? It is a long way down. Now Birbal, you have to do one thing for me."

Birbal replied, "Yes, Your Majesty."

Akbar said, "Well, I am your Emperor and so you have to obey me. By the time we reach the last step, you should be able to make me laugh. If you don't, then you will be punished to death."

Birbal had no choice but to obey. Birbal was not worried because he knew he could make Akbar laugh quite easily.

So he walked down the stairs with Emperor Akbar and started telling him a joke. But Akbar just did not laugh.

Birbal began to narrate another joke, then another, but Akbar would not laugh.

Birbal was not worried because there were yet many steps to go and he was sure that he would make Akbar laugh.

Birbal told many other jokes but it seemed that Akbar had quite made up his mind not to laugh at all. He would not even smile. Birbal then made funny faces but Akbar remained serious.

Now Birbal was really worried. They had come down the stairs and only a few steps remained. Birbal counted and found that there were ten steps left.

Akbar and Birbal

He quickly thought of other jokes but none would come to his mind. Then he just began making up his own jokes.

But Emperor Akbar was not amused. Birbal started feeling afraid because he knew that emperors could get people hanged easily. Sometimes even just because they were angry or upset.

Birbal started trembling as only five steps were left.

Now four steps were left. No jokes seemed to come to his mind. Just three steps were left. Birbal tried to tell a joke, but couldn't because he was really afraid now. So he kept silent.

They stepped on the second last step.

Birbal realised that his end was near because he couldn't make Akbar laugh. They were on the last step and Birbal could see his death very clearly now.

Out of fear, Birbal screamed at the Emperor, "You rogue. Why don't you laugh? Will you laugh only after you get me hanged?"

No one could speak so rudely to the Emperor. Birbal thought that now he would be surely punished to death.

But after hearing Birbal calling him a rogue and seeing his scared face, Akbar burst out laughing and went on laughing as he stepped down to the bottom of the stairs. Birbal was relieved.

Birbal apologised to his king but he realised that Akbar's timely laughter had saved him from a certain death.

Persia was a country far away from Agra. People who had been to Agra, told the Shah of Persia, many stories about the great Emperor Akbar and his minister, Birbal.

They all praised the witty and clever Birbal, and his ever ready answers.

The Shah of Persia was eager to meet Birbal and test him to see if he was really clever.

So the Shah sent a man to invite Birbal to Persia.

As Persia was far from Agra, the messenger took many months to reach Akbar's court. On reaching, he conveyed the Shah's invitation to Birbal.

Birbal took permission from Emperor Akbar and set off for Persia along with the messenger.

They reached Persia after a long journey and Birbal was asked to take some rest. The next day he was invited to meet the Shah.

In the court, he saw a strange scene. There were five people dressed in similar clothes, all like kings. They all sat on the same kind of thrones and they all behaved in the same manner.

The man with Birbal said, "Go and meet the Shah of Persia."

Birbal knew that he had to bow before the Shah and offer his respects but he had never seen the Shah before. How could he recognise the Shah as all the five men were dressed alike?

Akbar and Birbal

Birbal looked at the five men sitting on the thrones, from right to left and then left to right, again and again.

Then he went in front of one of them and greeted, "Oh! Great Shah of Persia! Emperor Akbar sends his regards and gifts for you, Your Highness. Have I guessed correctly that out of the five, you are the Shah of Persia?"

"Yes Birbal, you have guessed correctly. I did this to test you. You are really clever. I am the real Shah of Persia. Welcome to Persia. But tell me how did you recognise me?"

Birbal smiled and said, "Your Majesty. It was really quite simple. When I was looking at you, all these other four men looked at you to see your reaction as the subjects always look up to their king for everything. They looked at you wondering as to what you were thinking. But you were not looking at them. You were looking straight at me. So I knew that you are the real Shah of Persia."

"Birbal, you are really very clever," said the Shah of Persia. "I am so glad to meet you. Now I know why everyone always praises you. Well done Birbal."

The Shah of Persia then honoured Birbal with the title, 'Ocean of Intelligence', for being so clever and also presented him many gifts when Birbal returned to Akbar's court.

The clever and kind Birbal was liked a lot by most of the people in Akbar's court. But he also had some enemies. Two jealous courtiers went to the royal barber and said, "We have a plan. If you help us, we will give you a lot of money."

The barber was a greedy man so he agreed to do what the two men wanted.

The next day, the barber went to Emperor Akbar as planned.

He said to Akbar, "Your Majesty, I wonder how your ancestors are. Don't you ever worry about them? They must be angry with you for not thinking about them at all."

"My ancestors are dead and in heaven and I am alive. How can I find out how they are?" asked Akbar.

The barber said, "Your Majesty, you can send someone from here to find out about their well being."

"But how can I send anyone to heaven?" asked Akbar.

The barber said, "Your Majesty, get a thousand bundles of hay piled up in an open field. Then a person can stand on the pile of hay and the hay be set on fire. The man will go straight to heaven with the smoke."

"But whom can I send?" asked Akbar, beginning to sense something fishy.

"Birbal of course, Your Majesty. He is the cleverest of us all and will do the best job," said the barber.

Akbar knew that Birbal had some enemies but he trusted Birbal to find a solution to this problem too.

So Akbar called Birbal to the court and said, "Birbal, you have to go to heaven to see if my ancestors need anything."

Birbal said, "This is an excellent idea. You have thought well, Your Majesty."

"No Birbal, this is the idea of my clever barber," said Akbar.

Birbal understood and decided to teach the barber a lesson.

Birbal said, "Your Majesty, I will certainly go to heaven. But could I go after some days because I have a few important matters to settle?"

"Sure Birbal. You finish your work and go after a week," said Akbar.

Akbar ordered for a thousand bundles of hay to be collected on a field, which would be burnt to send Birbal to heaven. Akbar chose a field which was near Birbal's house.

Birbal asked some trusted men to dig a secret tunnel under the ground from the place where the hay was kept to his house, within seven days.

On the fixed day, people gathered to see Birbal go to heaven.

Birbal went and stood on the pile of hay. As the hay was put on fire, Birbal quickly slipped into the tunnel under the hay and ran home safely.

For six months, he hid in his house and did not meet anyone. He let his hair and beard grow.

His enemies rejoiced for they were happy to get rid of the clever Birbal.

After six months, Birbal left his house and went to the Emperor's court.

Akbar was very happy to have Birbal back safe and sound.

He welcomed Birbal and said, "How nice that you could go to heaven. Did you meet my ancestors?"

"Yes I did, Your Majesty," said Birbal.

"Tell me, how are they all? Are they comfortable in heaven?" asked Akbar.

Akbar and Birbal

"Yes, Your Majesty. They are really happy there and have no problems, except one," said Birbal.

"What is that? I will see to it that their problem is solved immediately," said Akbar.

"My Lord, there is no barber in the heaven. All your ancestors want you to do something about it," said Birbal.

"What do they want?" asked Akbar.

"They want a barber to be sent to cut their hair and give them a shave," said Birbal.

"But whom can I send?" asked Akbar.

Birbal said, "Your Majesty, your own barber would be the best to send."

Akbar ordered the royal barber to be burnt with hay just as Birbal.

The scared barber fell at Akbar's feet crying, "Mercy, Your Majesty. Don't burn me. I will die."

Birbal said, "No, you won't die. See I have come back from heaven."

The barber said, "I don't know how you came back but I will certainly be burnt to death. My Lord, I was forced to do this by Birbal's enemies."

Akbar was very angry and said, "No one can force a person to do anything bad. I think you just did all this for money."

Akbar then punished the two courtiers and the barber. The whole court applauded Birbal for his clever thinking.

Akbar and Birbal

A SEARCH FOR BIRBAL

One day, Emperor Akbar got angry with Birbal over something, and told him to leave his court and never come back.

Birbal went home thinking, "The Emperor is angry with me. If I stay here or in my country house, he might give me a heavier punishment."

Birbal decided to hide in an unknown place for sometime, so that the Emperor would start missing him.

Soon after, Akbar began to miss Birbal because with the clever Birbal around, he could talk about interesting things.

So he ordered that Birbal should be called back to the court. But Birbal was not to be found anywhere.

Akbar became very worried. He also got quite bored and wanted Birbal to come back to make his life more interesting and lively.

Akbar thought, "Where can Birbal go? He must be hiding in some far off village."

So one day, he thought of a plan to get Birbal back. He called all his messengers and told them to go to all the village chiefs around Agra and tell them to reach Agra within fifteen days.

Akbar said, "But tell all the chiefs that on the way to Agra, they have to walk partly in the sun and partly in the shade."

The chiefs found the order strange but none could defy the king's orders.

After a few days, Akbar saw the chiefs walking into the courtyard towards the court. Some of the chiefs had a piece of cloth on their heads. Some were actually trying to walk half in the sun and half in the shade formed by pillars.

But one man was carrying a cot, with his hands holding it over his head. It was a cot woven with jute ropes.

So wherever there were ropes, there was shade and through the gaps, the sun was shining on the man. It was half shade and half sunny under the cot.

Akbar asked his courtiers to bring that man to him.

Akbar said, "Very good, my man. You win. But tell me, who gave you this idea or you will be punished?"

The man said, "My Lord! The man is a friend's friend and has recently come to stay with him."

Akbar knew that Birbal was the only one who could have thought of this.

Akbar said, "Tell that stranger to come and see me at once. By the way, what is the stranger's name?"

The village chief said, "His name is Birbal but he won't come. He was saying that you are angry with him."

"I have pardoned Birbal and I am no longer angry with him. Tell him that he must come back at once to Agra. I am waiting for him to come back to the court as soon as possible," said Akbar.

When the village chief reached his village, he told Birbal what the Emperor had said. Birbal was happy to know that Akbar was no longer angry with him.

When Birbal came back to Agra, Akbar welcomed Birbal and said, "Birbal, see I have got you out of your hiding. This time I was cleverer than you."

Ali came running to the house of Birbal. He was a servant who worked for the Emperor and he looked very worried.

He shouted, "Birbal, My Lord, please save me or the Emperor will have me killed. Oh! Please save me Sir!"

Birbal said, "Ali, tell me what is the problem and I will try to help you."

26   *Akbar and Birbal*

The servant said, "Some time back, a holy man had gifted a parrot to the Emperor. The Emperor entrusted me with looking after the parrot. He had warned that anyone who informed him about the parrot's death would be sentenced to death. Alas! the parrot is dead."

"How did it die?" asked Birbal.

Ali said, "I don't know, Sir. I looked after it very well but when I got up in the morning, it was already dead."

Birbal promised, "Ali, I will see to it that you are not hanged for this."

Birbal went to Akbar and said, "Your Majesty, do you remember the parrot a holy man had given you?"

Akbar said, "Of course, Birbal. I do remember. I told my trusted servant, Ali to look after the parrot. But why are you asking me about the parrot?"

Birbal said, "Oh! Your Majesty. That parrot is really great. It is holy too."

Surprised, Akbar asked, "Birbal, how can a parrot be holy and great?"

Birbal said, "Yes, My Lord. The parrot is lying in a state of meditation. It is thinking and not doing anything else."

Akbar said, "I want to see that parrot at once." They all walked to Ali's house where the parrot was lying motionless.

Akbar looked at it and said, "What foolishness is this Birbal? The parrot is not thinking. It is dead, isn't it?"

Birbal bowed, "Please forgive me for this, My Lord. I had seen that the parrot was dead but I was afraid."

Akbar said, "Birbal! Afraid! Why?"

Birbal said, "My Lord. You had said that the person who gave the news of the parrot's death would be sentenced to death. I did this just to save my life. Ali was also very frightened."

Akbar said, "Now I remember what I had said. Don't worry. Nobody will be sentenced to death for this. Call Ali."

Ali came and bowed in front of Akbar saying, "My Lord. I really looked after the parrot well. I don't know how it died. I am very sorry but please trust me."

Akbar forgave him saying, "Ali, it does not matter. The parrot must have died a natural death. I know that I can trust you."

When Ali found Birbal alone, Ali said, "Oh, My Lord! Thank you so much. You have saved my life. Only you could have saved me. You are so clever and intelligent. God bless you, Sir."

A MOTHER'S BEAUTIFUL CHILD

Akbar once said to his courtiers, "I think that my grandson, Khurram is really a beautiful child. What do you all think?"

The courtiers wanted to please Akbar, so they all said, "Your Highness, Prince Khurram is the most beautiful child."

Birbal kept sitting quietly.

Akbar asked him, "What is the matter Birbal? You don't seem to agree with me and the others in the court. Don't you find my Khurram to be the most beautiful child?"

Birbal stood up and bowed before Akbar and said, "I think it is very difficult to test what is beautiful and what is not. There is no real test for beauty."

Akbar felt bad and said, "No Birbal, I do not agree with you. A rose is beautiful and a crow ugly to all."

Wanting to prove Birbal wrong, Akbar then said to all the courtiers, "I order each of you to bring a child each to find the most beautiful child of all."

The next day, all the courtiers, except Birbal, brought a child each.

After looking at all the children, Akbar said, "I still think that my grandson, Khurram is the best looking."

Akbar asked Birbal, "Why have you not brought a child, Birbal?"

"I could not find any child who was perfect," said Birbal.

Akbar asked, "Birbal, you still don't agree that my Khurram is the most handsome out of all the children?"

"Please give me some time. I will have to search for one," said Birbal.

"As you wish, Birbal," Akbar replied.

The next day, Birbal said, "Your Majesty, I have at last found the most beautiful child in Agra, but the mother will not let the child come here because she loves the child a lot."

Akbar said, "We will go to her house and see the child there."

Akbar ordered the courtiers to accompany him to see the child. Everyone quickly got ready to leave, for they all were eager to see the most beautiful child, as Birbal had claimed. Then they started walking, with Birbal leading the way.

They soon reached the slums where the poor people lived.

Then Birbal stopped and said, "This is where the child lives. We will wait here for some time."

In a short while, a child crawled out from a hut. The courtiers looked at Birbal with surprise because the child was not beautiful at all. Rather the child was the ugliest of all the children the courtiers had brought, and this made Akbar angry.

Akbar shouted, "Birbal! What kind of a joke is this? The child is ugly."

Birbal replied patiently, "Just wait a while, please."

They kept standing for some time watching the child playing. Suddenly, the child fell and started crying.

A woman came running out of the hut and said, "Oh my dear child, my poor darling, are you hurt?"

The child continued crying and the woman spoke to the child, "Hush, my beautiful child. Don't cry. You are the apple of my eye. No one is as lovely as you are. I love you more than anything else."

A courtier exclaimed, "Oh Lord! How can she call this ugly child beautiful?"

The mother of the child heard this and she shouted, "Are you speaking about my child?"

The courtier replied, "We are speaking the truth. Your child is ugly."

The mother screamed loudly, "How dare you talk about my child like this?"

"Go and search the whole world and you will not find a child more beautiful than mine. Go away from here and dare not speak like that about my child."

Akbar indicated his courtiers to leave. He turned to Birbal and said, "You have proved your point, Birbal. You have proved that everyone thinks that their child is the most beautiful."

Birbal smiled and said, "Not only child, Your Majesty, even grandchild!"

Akbar started laughing and said, "Birbal you are right. I find Khurram to be the most beautiful for he is my own. Every parent finds his child to be the most beautiful."

THE ROOT OF THE PROBLEM

People trusted Birbal so they often came to him with their problems. One day, a man came running up to Birbal and fell at his feet saying, "Sir, someone has stolen all my money."

Birbal saw how upset the poor man was but he asked, "You are wearing dirty clothes. You look poor, then how can you have money?"

The man said, "Sir, I work very hard in the gardens of the Emperor so that I can save money for my old age, as I have no one to look after me. I had saved a thousand gold coins but someone has stolen them. I am ruined."

"First tell me where the money was kept," asked Birbal.

"As I work in the gardens of the king, I dug a hole under a pear tree and kept all my money there. But all of it is gone," said the gardener, and started crying.

"Crying will not help you. Stop crying and let me think," said Birbal.

Birbal thought, "The money was in the hole under a pear tree. Who would dig up over there?"

Suddenly, things were clear in Birbal's mind and he said to the gardener, "Go home. I will soon get your money back. But be careful next time and don't keep the money in such an unsafe place. I won't help you if you act so carelessly again."

Birbal summoned all the doctors of the city and asked them about the benefits of the pear tree. He finally asked them, "Does the pear tree help in making any medicines?"

They said, "No."

But one doctor replied, "The fruits and leaves do not help us but the roots have medicinal value."

Birbal asked, "Have you used the roots of the pear tree for any medicine?"

The doctor replied, "Yes, My Lord. Just a few days back, I made a medicine from the roots of the pear tree. It cured a patient of mine who was very ill."

"Who was that man whom you cured? Go and fetch him," ordered Birbal.

The man came and Birbal asked, "Has this doctor been treating you?"

"Yes Sir, and I am well because of the wonderful medicine he made from the roots of the pear tree," said the man.

"From where did you get the roots for the medicine?" asked Birbal.

"I sent my servant to get it, Sir," said the man. So Birbal ordered him to get the servant. The man left at once and came back with the servant.

Birbal asked, "So you helped to cure your master?"

"Yes, Sir. I brought the roots of the pear tree for the medicine," said the servant.

"Where was the tree?" asked Birbal.

"In the king's garden," said the man.

"Give me the thousand coins at once that you found while digging for the roots under the pear tree," said Birbal.

The scared servant said, "Yes, Sir. I will give it back. I have stolen the bag of gold coins and that was a wrong thing to do. Please pardon me."

"Go get the money, then you will not be punished. You had stolen the money and that was wrong. Since you have confessed, I forgive you."

The servant ran to get the money and soon gave the bag of thousand gold coins to Birbal.

Then Birbal gave five gold coins to the servant and said, "You can keep these coins for speaking the truth."

The servant fell at Birbal's feet and said, "Thank you so much, My Lord. I promise never to steal again."

Birbal then said to the gardener, "Take your money. I have taken out five gold coins because you were stupid enough to keep your money in an unsafe place. Be careful in the future."

One day Akbar got angry with his Empress and ordered her to leave his palace immmediately.

The Empress tried to speak, but Akbar would not listen. "Go away. You may, however, take with you, whatever is dear to you but leave my palace now."

41

The Empress was very upset and did not know what to do. Then she thought of Birbal and had him called. When Birbal came, she told him all that had happened.

Birbal said, "The Emperor said that you could take what was dear to you. Is that right, Your Highness?"

"Yes," said the Empress.

Birbal told his plan to the Empress and went away. The Empress told her maids to pack her clothes.

When the packing was done, she asked her maid to tell Akbar to come and meet her as she was going. Akbar came and stood silently. He was still angry and would not speak with her.

The Empress said, "Don't talk if you don't want to, but have this juice."

Birbal had asked the Empress to put a sleeping pill in the juice. Akbar felt drowsy after drinking it and fell asleep.

Birbal had planned everything already. The sleeping Emperor was carefully carried to a palanquin.

With the sleeping Emperor in the palanquin, the Empress left with her bodyguards for her father's house.

When they reached her father's house, he was very surprised but glad to have them come to stay with him. Akbar was carried to a room and laid on a bed.

Her father was worried to see the sleeping Akbar being carried to bed, but the Empress said, "Don't worry, Father. He will wake up in an hour."

When Akbar woke up, he was shocked to see where he was. Angrily, he shouted at his wife, who was standing nearby, "How did I come here?"

The Empress said, "Don't be angry, Your Majesty, but I was just obeying your orders."

Akbar said, "What do you mean?"

His wife said, "When you asked me to leave the palace, you had said that I could take with me whatever was dear to me. Well, you are the dearest of all to me, so I brought you with me."

Forgetting his anger, Akbar burst out laughing.

He said, "You are very clever, my dear wife."

"No, actually this was Birbal's clever thinking," confessed the Empress.

Akbar said, "Birbal! I should have known. We are so lucky to have him. His clever thinking got us together. God bless him."

Akbar and Birbal

THE OBEDIENT HUSBANDS

One day Akbar and Birbal were roaming the streets of Agra, dressed like common men. Akbar would often roam the streets in a disguise to see if the people in his kingdom were happy or not, and if they had any problems.

As they were walking along, they heard a woman shouting at her husband, "You are good for nothing. Go away and come back only when you have proved your worth."

Akbar and Birbal saw that the wife was short and thin but the husband was tall and strong. Yet the husband was quietly listening to his wife's scolding.

Akbar asked, "Why doesn't the husband shout back at his wife?"

Birbal said, "The husband has to listen without shouting back. This is nothing new, My Lord. Please believe me. Every husband listens to his wife. This is the real truth of marriage."

The next day when the courtiers came into the court, Akbar told them, "All the married men come in front and all those, who are not married, stay behind."

All the married men stepped forward.

Akbar then said, "All right. Now all the husbands who listen to their wives should step to my right. Those who don't obey their wives should step to my left."

Akbar was shocked when all, but one man moved towards their right. It meant that Birbal was right.

Akbar said, "Birbal, you were wrong."

Birbal replied, "Your Majesty, let me first ask this man a question. Why did you not join the others?"

"Sir, I was about to go with the others and then I remembered that my wife had told me not to go with the crowd. So I stayed away from the crowd."

Everyone burst out laughing and Akbar said, "So you listen to your wife too. All right, I believe you, Birbal. You have again proved that you are right. All husbands do listen to their wives."

BLIND EYES

The Empress came to her husband, Emperor Akbar and said, "My Lord, I want to donate charity to each and every blind person in the city."

Akbar ordered for a list of all the blind men in the city to be made. The list was prepared within a day and given to Akbar.

Akbar said, "I think the courtiers could prepare the list so soon because there are very few blind people in our city."

Birbal said, "But, Your Majesty, I have to say one thing. More than the blind people, there are many people who have eyesight, yet cannot see."

Akbar did not believe him, so Birbal said, "I will prove myself right in a few days."

After some days, Birbal sat on the roadside stringing jute ropes on a cot.

Two men, passing by, asked him, "What are you doing, Birbal?"

Birbal had a clerk standing next to him. He said, "Start writing one, two."

The clerk wrote as asked. As Birbal continued stringing the cot, more people asked, "What are you doing?" and Birbal continued his counting, "Eightyone, eightytwo, eightythree."

Soon this news reached the palace and Akbar too came to see for himself, what Birbal was up to.

Akbar saw Birbal stringing the cot.

He could not understand why Birbal was doing this, so he also asked, "Birbal, what are you doing?"

Birbal did not look at Akbar. He went on stringing the cot and spoke out, "Two hundred and fifty."

Birbal stopped stringing the cot and took the paper with the numbers from the clerk and gave it to Akbar saying, "Your Highness, I had promised that I will give you the list of people who had eyes but could not see. Here are two hundred and fifty names of such people. Please see it. Each of these people could see me stringing the jute in broad daylight, yet asked me what I was doing."

Akbar said, "That is good. I am convinced now. Let me see the list."

Akbar went through the list as everyone stood silently. Then Akbar suddenly shouted, "Birbal, why have you written my name here?"

Birbal smiled and said, "Your Majesty. You were the last one to come and ask me what I was doing."

Akbar laughed, saying, "Very true, Birbal. I did ask you that question."

One day when Birbal came late to the court, everyone turned towards him and started laughing. He could make out that they had been making fun of him.

Akbar said, "Birbal, we were discussing that all of us are fair, then why is it that you have a darker skin?"

Birbal replied, "That's true, My Lord. Actually, there is a secret behind this which no one knows."

Then Akbar said angrily, "Birbal, have you kept a secret from me, even your Emperor? I order you to tell it to me."

Birbal replied politely, "I will do as you say, Your Majesty. I will have to tell you about something from the past."

Akbar said, "Tell us. We really want to know." All the courtiers agreed.

Then Birbal explained, "God created the world. God felt something was amiss, so He made plants, birds and animals."

Akbar said, "That is no secret."

Birbal said, "But still God was not happy, so God made man. Then He felt happy and thought of bestowing gifts upon all of us."

Akbar asked, "What gifts, Birbal?"

Birbal replied, "God threw money, looks and brains down on the earth. He gave five minutes to all to pick up as many gifts as they could."

Then Akbar asked, "So? What happened then?"

"My secret is that I spent all the five minutes in gathering wit and cleverness, and did not have time for the other two. But all of you were busy in picking up looks and money. This is my secret."

Many courtiers felt bad because they knew that Birbal had in a way said that they were not clever. But Akbar laughed loudly, appreciating Birbal's clever reply.

53

A LIST OF FOOLS

Birbal was once ordered by Akbar to prepare a list of fools in the city of Agra.

Birbal went around the city looking for people and adding their names to his list of fools, wherever and whenever he saw them doing something foolish.

Meanwhile, a man came to the court to sell a horse to Akbar. Akbar was highly impressed with the fine horse.

The man said, "My Lord, I have a hundred such horses to sell. If you want to buy them, then I will get them for you."

Akbar said, "Yes, I want to buy the horses. Why did you not bring all of them with you?"

The horse dealer replied, "It would have cost me a lot of money to bring them with me. But if you give me a lakh gold coins, then I can bring all of them in fifteen days."

The horse dealer was given the lakh gold coins from the royal treasury and he left promising to come back soon.

After a few days, Birbal returned from his search for fools. Akbar was so happy with the horse he had bought, that he took Birbal with him to the horse.

Akbar showed the horse and asked, "Isn't this horse wonderful?"

Birbal agreed that it was a fine horse. Akbar said proudly, "I will be getting a hundred such horses in fifteen days."

Birbal asked, "But from where will you get such hundred horses?"

Akbar said, "The horse dealer who gave me this horse will bring hundred more such horses for me. I have given him a lakh of gold coins for the horses."

Birbal asked surprisingly, "You have already given that money? Your Majesty, do you know who he is? Do you know where he lives? Does anybody know him?"

"No," said Akbar.

Birbal said, "Then how can you be sure, Your Majesty, that the man is honest and will bring those horses?"

Akbar said, "Well, he looked honest and I am sure he will come back."

Birbal asked, "But if he doesn't?"

Akbar said, "Oh, stop it! He will bring the horses. Now forget all this. Tell me, have you made the list of fools?"

Birbal said, "It is almost ready."

Birbal wrote something on the list. Then he gave it to Akbar and stood quietly.

Akbar started reading and then shouted, "Birbal, why is my name on the very top of the list of fools?"

Birbal said, "Your Majesty, just think over it. A stranger comes and brings a horse, and you give him a lakh of gold coins. Isn't that foolishness?"

Akbar said, "But how can you say just now that I am a fool? That man may come back with the horses."

Birbal said, "But we don't know, My Lord. What if he doesn't come back?"

Akbar said, "But Birbal, what if the man does come back in fifteen days with all the hundred horses?"

Birbal said, "He won't, My Lord."

Akbar said, "But what if he does? Then you will be proved wrong, Birbal?"

Birbal said, "Then I will cut your name from the top of the list of fools."

Akbar said, "Oh, that is good!"

Birbal said, "But I will write the name of the horse dealer in that place."

Akbar said, "You mean that if the horse dealer comes to give me the hundred horses, then he will be a bigger fool than everyone whose names are written here."

Birbal said, "Quite right, Your Majesty."

Akbar could not help laughing at Birbal's ever ready wit.

THE DAUGHTER OF BIRBAL

One day, Birbal's daughter asked her father to take her to the court of Akbar. She was very young and wanted to see the palace of Akbar.

Birbal took her to the palace and then she went around all the gardens and saw all the rooms of the palace.

She lived in a big house herself because her father, Birbal was a minister in Akbar's court, but she found that everything was more grand and beautiful in Akbar's huge palace.

When she had seen everything, she was taken to the court of Akbar.

Birbal introduced her to Akbar. On Akbar's orders, she was given wonderful things to eat and drink.

Then Akbar started talking to her. He asked, "Did you like my palace?"

She just nodded her head.

Akbar picked her up and made her sit on his lap. Then he asked, "Do you know how to talk?"

She nodded and said, "Yes, Your Majesty. Neither less nor more."

Akbar asked, "What do you mean?"

She replied, "I talk less with elders and more with my friends."

Akbar laughed and said, "Birbal, your daughter has given such a quick reply. She is just like you, clever and witty."

Akbar was getting ready for the court. As he was being dressed, his grandson came running to him.

Akbar's grandson sat on his lap and said, "There is something on your moustache. Bend down, Grandpa and I will remove it." Akbar bent down and Khurram pulled one hair from his white moustache.

Akbar shouted, "Ooooh! You naughty boy! What have you done?"

Khurram ran away shouting, "See Grandpa, I have fooled you."

Akbar walked to his court and thought, "I must put this question to my courtiers and see what they answer. Oh, I will enjoy myself! This time even Birbal will not be able to answer."

Akbar then questioned his courtiers, "Someone pulled out one hair from my moustache. I want you all to guess his name and tell me what kind of punishment should be given to that person."

The courtiers were unable to guess the person's name. They wondered as to who could have dared to pull a hair from their Emperor's moustache?

One courtier shouted, "Whosoever it may be, that person should be jailed."

Another courtier said, "Put him under an elephant's legs."

Others shouted, "Hang him, My Lord."

Akbar was very happy that no one had been able to guess the culprit's name.

Akbar saw that Birbal was very quiet.

Akbar thought, "Well, this time even Birbal does not know the answer, that is why he is not answering."

Akbar said, "Birbal, why have you not yet suggested any punishment?"

"I think, Your Majesty, you should give that person a kiss," Birbal said confidently.

Akbar thought, "This answer shows that Birbal has understood who pulled my moustache hair. He is really very clever. I can never defeat him." But the other courtiers were shocked.

"What are you saying?" asked one.

"Are you out of your mind?" said another.

Akbar asked, "A kiss is given as a reward, not as a punishment, Birbal. Why do you want me to reward and not punish the culprit?"

Birbal said, "Your Highness, you don't need to give any punishment. No one can dare to pull out a hair of your moustache because you are the King."

"But I am telling the truth, someone has done that," Akbar insisted.

Birbal said, "Yes, I know that, Your Majesty. But I think that only a child could have had done it. And that also your own grandson whom you love so much. So you should give him a kiss."

Akbar said, "You are right again, Birbal. It was Khurram who playfully pulled the hair from my moustache."

A CHARIOT FOR BIRBAL

Akbar was very busy in the court, when a messenger came and said, "My Lord, the Queen wants you to meet her now."

Akbar said, "Tell her that I am busy."

After sometime, the messenger came again and said, "Your Highness, the Queen wants you to meet her at once."

Akbar got off the throne to go to his wife. As he was going, he saw Birbal smile, which annoyed him.

Akbar shouted at Birbal, "This smile is an insult to me. How dare you make fun of me, Birbal! You must be punished for this."

Birbal stood up as Akbar ordered, "Go away from here at once, and never ever put your foot on this ground."

Birbal walked out and went home. For many days, no one saw Birbal in the court. Actually, they didn't see him anywhere. Even Akbar began missing Birbal, for he always made him laugh.

One day, Akbar was standing by the window when he saw Birbal on a chariot. He shouted to a servant, "Go and call Birbal at once."

The servant ran outside. Birbal did not come inside but brought his chariot near the window where Akbar was standing.

Akbar pretended to be angry and said, "Birbal, why are you here? I told you not to put your foot here again."

Birbal said, "I am following your orders, Your Majesty."

"I told you to go but you have come back. You did not obey me," said Akbar.

Birbal said, "My Lord, you had said that I should not put my foot on your ground ever again. I am obeying you."

"But you are in the city," said Akbar.

"I am on a chariot, Your Majesty and not on the ground," said Birbal.

"So what?" asked Akbar.

Birbal said, "Your Majesty, 'ground' also means soil. So I went to the next kingdom and got soil from there."

"Why?" asked Akbar.

Birbal said, "I spread the soil of the other kingdom on the floor of the chariot. Now my feet rest on the soil of another kingdom and not your empire."

Akbar asked, "And when you get off?"

Birbal said, "I don't get off this chariot at all. I live on this chariot because I don't want to leave your kingdom and go anywhere. On the chariot, I will be in your kingdom but not on your ground."

Akbar said, "Your answer has touched me, Birbal. I take back my words. I forgive you. Now you need not stay on a chariot. Come down."

So with the clever-witted Birbal back, the court was full of life again.

A stranger was brought to the court. He bowed in front of Akbar and very politely said, "My respects to you."

Akbar asked, "Who are you and where do you come from?"

The stranger replied, "My Lord, I am a master of many languages like Arabic, Persian and Sanskrit."

He continued, "I have heard that in your court, there are many clever and learned people. I would want them to tell you where I am from."

Akbar said, "But how will they know where you are from?"

The man said, "From the way a person speaks, others can make out the place one belongs to. Can anyone here guess the place I belong to?"

Akbar said, "Yes, of course. There are many people in my kingdom who are wise and will be able to find out. Meanwhile, be my guest and stay in the palace."

Akbar ordered the learned people of his kingdom to find out where the man was from. These people talked for a long time with the stranger.

Then one of them said to Akbar, "Your Majesty, he speaks many languages so fluently that we cannot make out the place he belongs to."

Akbar then turned to Birbal and said, "Do you have anything to say, Birbal."

Akbar continued, "Can't you find out, Birbal?"

Birbal replied confidently, "I will tell you tomorrow morning, Your Majesty."

As planned, at night, Birbal's loyal servant quietly entered the room where the stranger was sleeping. He splashed some water on the sleeping man's face.

The man got up with a start, speaking loudly.

Birbal, who had been hiding in the room all this while, heard the stranger speak and quietly left the room.

Next day in the court, Akbar looked at Birbal hopefully.

Akbar asked, "Birbal, could you find out where this man comes from?"

Birbal said, "Yes, My Lord, I am sure that he is from Gujarat."

The surprised stranger said, "That is true but how did you find out?"

Birbal smiled and said, "When a person is angry, in pain or surprised, he will always talk in his mother tongue. Last night, while you were sleeping, my servant sprinkled some water on you and you got up suddenly, shouting in Gujarati."

The stranger turned to Birbal and said, "That was really very clever. You are truly wise and intelligent, Birbal."

Everyone nodded with a smile, agreeing with the stranger.

Akbar said, "Birbal, I am happy that you have kept the honour of our kingdom."

WHOSE BAD LUCK WAS IT?

Everyone believed that servant Gulshan was unlucky. If anyone saw him, the first thing in the morning, then the whole day would be full of bad luck.

One morning, Akbar woke up earlier than usual. Seeing no one around Akbar called out, "Is any one there?"

Gulshan was working just outside the room, but he did not dare to go in front of Akbar because he knew that people considered him unlucky. He did not want Akbar to see his face, the first thing in the morning.

Akbar shouted again, "Any one there? Come here at once."

Gulshan felt he should obey the Emperor as no one was around and so he went in. He bent low saluting Akbar.

Akbar saw his face and thought, "My goodness! Gulshan is an unlucky man. I hope my day goes well."

Akbar said to Gulshan, "Call the other servants and tell them to help me get ready."

Gulshan saluted and went outside and sent the other servants in. As he was getting ready, a servant came and said, "My Lord, Prince Khurram is very ill. He is crying and asking for you."

Akbar rushed to see Khurram.

After some time, the royal doctor said, "Your Highness, the prince is better now. His fever has come down. There is no danger. There is nothing to worry now."

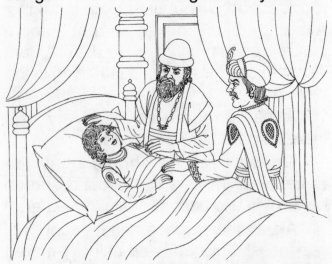

Just then, a servant said, "Your Highness, it is very late and you have not eaten breakfast. Please come and eat first."

As Akbar sat to eat, a messenger came running and said, "The ambassador from Burma has been waiting for you since morning."

Akbar said, "All right, I am coming."

Akbar spent time discussing important matters with him. Later, as Akbar bade farewell to the ambassador, one of his ministers came and whispered in his ear, "Your Majesty, I have bad news. There has been a rebellion against you."

Akbar said, "Quickly go, and call the Commander of the army of that area."

It was a very serious matter and they kept planning till late that evening. Akbar was very tired and hungry.

Akbar ordered for food to be laid and as he sat down to eat, he got a severe pain in his stomach.

The royal doctor was summoned. The doctor examined Akbar and gave him some bitter medicines to swallow.

He then said, "My Lord, kindly do not eat anything for an hour or two."

Akbar suddenly thought, "What a bad day. Could it be because I had seen that unlucky man, Gulshan, in the morning? A man like him should not live."

Next day, Akbar announced in his court, "I order Gulshan to be put to death."

Birbal felt very bad that a man was being put to death just because he was considered unlucky.

Birbal went straight to Akbar and said, "Your Majesty, please do not punish Gulshan. He has committed no crime."

Akbar said, "Gulshan is unlucky for everyone. I myself suffered yesterday when I saw his face in the morning. He must die. Such men should not live."

Birbal said, "If you permit, I would like to ask him some questions."

Akbar agreed and ordered for Gulshan to be summoned to the court.

A scared Gulshan walked in and quietly stood in a corner.

Birbal asked, "Gulshan, yesterday whose face did you see first?"

Gulshan said politely, "I saw the Emperor's face, My Lord."

"Are you sure?" asked Birbal.

Gulshan replied, "Yes, My Lord."

Birbal turned towards Akbar and said, "Your Majesty, you believe that seeing Gulshan's face first thing in the morning brought you bad luck. Isn't it?"

Akbar just nodded.

Birbal said, "What if Gulshan says that seeing your face brought him bad luck because now he has to die."

Akbar felt ashamed of himself and said, "You are right, Birbal. I was wrong. You have saved me from the sin of sentencing an innocent man to death."

Akbar apologised to Gulshan and announced that Gulshan would no longer be considered unlucky. Gulshan fell at Birbal's feet and thanked him for saving his life.

Akbar and Birbal

In the good olden days, kings would often disguise themselves and mingle with the common men of their kingdom. They would do this to find out if the subjects were happy with the king and his rule, and if they had any grievances. Even Akbar loved to roam around his city in disguise to find about his people.

Birbal, as a friend and Akbar's minister, often advised Akbar not to go out alone for it could be dangerous, but Akbar would not listen.

One day, Birbal said, "Your Majesty, your life is very precious for all of us, so it is not safe for you to go alone. Please, let me come with you."

Akbar said, "You worry a lot, Birbal. I am going now. Nothing will happen."

Akbar left the palace for the areas where the common people lived.

Later, seeing a man following him, Akbar thought, "Why is this man following me? What if he tries to harm me?"

Akbar started walking fast and so did the man behind. Suddenly, Akbar stopped and the man stopped too.

Again Akbar started walking and the man followed. When Akbar looked back, the man stopped walking and started looking here and there.

Akbar got angry and walked straight to the man who had been following him.

Akbar asked him angrily, "What is your name?"

The man replied, "Wanderlust."

Akbar said, "What do you do?"

The man said, "I wander."

Akbar was getting angrier and he asked, "Where do you live?"

The man replied rudely, "Everywhere."

Akbar was not used to anyone talking like this to him. He felt very angry and said, "How dare you talk to me like this! Do you know who I am?"

The man replied, "What is so special about you? You are an ordinary man just like me and the others."

Akbar shouted angrily, "No! I am Emperor Akbar."

"Bah! How can that be? Just look at your clothes," said the man casually.

"I am the great Emperor Akbar. Do you want proof? This is the royal ring I am wearing. Now do you believe me that I am Akbar?"

The man said, "Anyone can get an expensive ring made and call himself the king. I don't believe you. However, I may believe you if you show me the seal ring."

Akbar took off the government seal ring and held in his palm to show it to the man. The man quickly snatched the ring from Akbar's hand and ran away from there.

Akbar was shocked that the man had stolen the seal ring. For a moment he stood still. He regained his composure for he knew how important the seal was.

He started shouting, "Thief! Thief! Catch him."

Some people standing nearby heard Akbar and started running after the thief.

The thief was running fast but soon the people caught him. Akbar was still far behind when he was caught.

As Akbar neared the crowd, he heard the thief shout, "Keep your hands off me. I am your Emperor. If you don't believe me, see the royal ring, with the government seal."

The people saw the ring and got scared. They had dared to hit their Emperor and were scared that they might be punished for this foolish act of theirs.

They fell at the man's feet pleading, "Pardon us, Your Highness. We are sorry. We did not recognise you. Please forgive us. A man was calling you a thief. We will beat him. Where is he?"

Akbar stopped at a distance from the crowd. He knew now that no one would believe him and that if he went closer, then people might start hitting him.

Akbar rushed back to the palace and quickly went to his royal chambers. Akbar was very worried for he had lost the seal ring.

He kept pacing in his room, thinking of ways to get his ring back.

Akbar thought of Birbal. "Birbal would know what to do. But I cannot go to him because he had warned me not to go out alone. Oh Lord! What should I do?"

Akbar felt thirsty and was about to pick up the glass of water, when to his surprise he saw his ring lying on the table.

He picked up the ring and quickly slid it into his finger.

"Oh, how wonderful!" he thought, for he was glad to have the ring back. His eyes then fell on a letter lying on the ground.

Akbar thought, "The thief must have returned this ring and written this letter to apologise for his misdeed."

But the letter did not have the word, 'sorry' at all. On it was written:

"Hadn't I warned you that it was not safe for you to go out alone in the city? You just lost the seal ring. Worse things could have happened to you – Birbal."

He felt angry that Birbal had been behind all this. But then he realised that had some thief actually followed him, then matters could have been worse.

Akbar smiled as he thought, "I should have known that the man following me was Birbal. What a good actor he is!"

Akbar sat down and thought, "Birbal is really wise. He certainly fooled me. But thank God, I have got this important ring back. I have learnt my lesson."

Akbar and Birbal

WHERE IS THE DONKEY?

Akbar had a long and tiring day at court, so he wanted to relax.

He said to his courtiers, "Tell me the difference between you all and a donkey."

One surprised courtier looked around the court and said, "But, My Lord, there are no donkeys here."

Everyone laughed at the courtier for being so foolish as to look around for a real, living donkey in the court.

Seeing Birbal quiet, Akbar said, "Aha! So this time even Birbal does not have an answer."

Birbal was still silent but he seemed to be working out something in his mind. He got up and walked to Akbar as if to measure the distance between Akbar and where he had been sitting.

Everyone was eagerly waiting for his answer.

Birbal said, "Your Majesty, the difference is about eight feet distance."

Akbar said, "Oh! I am sitting at about eight feet away from you. So you find me to be as foolish as a donkey."

Birbal stood quietly. All the other courtiers looked at Birbal with their mouths wide open. They wondered at his guts to call Akbar a donkey.

As ever, instead of getting angry, Akbar burst out laughing, saying, "Birbal, you are invincible. Nobody can match your wit."

One day, after the court proceedings, Akbar, feeling tired, was about to retire for the day, when a guard came to him.

The guard said, "A learned priest and thinker has come and wants to meet you and Minister Birbal. He is waiting outside."

Akbar, who had great regard for learned men, said, "Learned men should not be kept waiting. Go, call him in."

Akbar said, "Birbal, I am tired. Try to get this visit of the priest over soon."

Birbal replied, "Yes, My Lord. As you wish."

Akbar welcomed the priest with great respect. Then he asked the priest the purpose of his visit.

The priest said, "I want to test Birbal for his cleverness."

Birbal bowed and said, "I am ready, Sir."

The priest began, "Should I ask you a hundred easy questions or one difficult question?"

Aware that Akbar was tired, Birbal replied, "Ask me one difficult question."

The priest then asked, "What came first, the hen or the egg?"

Birbal replied quickly, "The hen."

The priest asked, "How can you say that?"

Birbal answered politely, "Sir, you had said that you will ask me one question."

The priest agreed, "That is right."

"Have I answered it?" Birbal asked.

"That is right too," said the priest.

"Then how can you ask me a second question?" asked Birbal.

The priest was very quiet for a minute, but then he said, "That is really very clever of you, Birbal. No, I cannot ask another question. You are right."

The priest turned to Akbar and said, "I had heard a lot about the clever Birbal and today, I affirm the fact that he is the cleverest of us all."

One day, Akbar felt angry because he needed Birbal in the court but he was not there and came late. After he came to the court, he went straight to Emperor Akbar.

Birbal bowed and said, "Your Majesty, please pardon me. I am sorry, I am late."

Akbar was so happy to see Birbal that he said, "It does not matter. There must have been something very important. But just tell me, why are you late, Birbal?"

Birbal said, "Well, My Lord. My four years old son's toy broke and he would not let me go till it was mended."

Akbar laughed and said, "So you came late to the court because you cannot manage a four-year-old child?"

Birbal stood quietly as everyone started making fun of his incapability to manage one small child.

Birbal said, "Sometimes small children can be very difficult to handle."

Akbar did not agree. He said, "Bring your four-year-old child here and I will handle him myself. Then learn from me how a child should be managed."

The next day, Birbal brought his four-year-old son to the court and leaving him with Akbar, went away for a while.

After the usual greetings, Akbar asked, "Well, son, what would you like to eat?"

The child said boldly, "A sugarcane."

Akbar ordered a sugarcane to be cut and brought for the child so that the child could eat it with ease. When the cut pieces of sugarcane were given to the child, he said, "Why have you cut this?"

Akbar asked, "How do you want it?"

The child said, "I want a full stick."

Akbar ordered the servant, "Immediately take this cut sugarcane and quickly bring another uncut stick."

The child interrupted, "No. I want this sugarcane only and none other."

"But just now you said that you wanted a whole stick," said Akbar.

"Yes, one whole stick. Join these cut pieces back because I want only this sugarcane," said the child adamantly.

Akbar said, "But that is not possible. Take another whole stick."

The child started crying loudly saying, "I want this sugarcane only. Join the cut pieces. It is your fault. Why did you cut it? I want only this sugarcane and none other." By now the child had started howling.

Akbar said, "My dear child, ask for anything else and I will give it to you but this sugarcane cannot be joined."

But the child would not listen. Completely fed up with the adamant child, Akbar sent for Birbal.

When Birbal came to pick up the child, Akbar said, "Birbal, you were very right. Sometimes, a child can be very difficult to please."

AKBAR AND THE LORD

A courtier wanting to flatter Emperor Akbar, said to him, "Your Majesty, you are the greatest, even greater than God."

Akbar said, "No, no. You are just praising me to make me feel good."

The courtier assured, "No, Your Majesty. I really mean it. I am only saying what I feel is the truth."

Later, when Akbar retired to his room at the end of the day, he wondered, "Am I really greater than God?"

Unable to arrive at any conclusion, he went off to sleep.

The next morning, he asked his courtiers, "Do you all also believe that I am greater than God Himself?"

Now the courtiers were a worried lot. They thought that if they said, "No, you are not greater than God," then Akbar could get angry.

To please Akbar, they all cried out in unison, "Yes, Your Majesty, there is no doubt that you are greater than God."

Akbar saw Birbal standing quietly, so he said, "You don't seem to agree with the others, Birbal. Do you think I am greater than God?"

Birbal stood up and said loudly and clearly, "Of course, you are, My Lord."

"What! Are you also trying to please me?" asked Akbar.

Birbal said, "No, My Lord."

Akbar felt very happy for he always believed Birbal.

Akbar asked Birbal the reason for his belief.

Birbal said, "You are greater, My Lord, because you can do one thing that even God cannot do."

Akbar asked, "Birbal, what is that?"

98   *Akbar and Birbal*

Birbal replied, "My Lord, if you are annoyed with someone, you can order him to leave your kingdom. But God cannot order anyone out of his kingdom?"

Akbar understood what Birbal was trying to say. He said, "Birbal, you believe that God cannot send anyone away from His kingdom because the whole universe belongs to God. Everything is under Him, the sky, the land, everything in the world."

"That is right, My Lord," said Birbal.

Akbar said, "But I can send people away because my kingdom on land is smaller than God's."

Akbar added, "Birbal, all these people were afraid to tell me the truth that God is greater than me, except you."

Birbal nodded but kept quiet.

Akbar said, "Birbal, you found a very novel way of making me realise that I am a mere humble being in front of God. I am grateful to you for making me see the truth. It was foolish of me to get carried away with false praise. Thank you so much Birbal."

Many courtiers were jealous of Birbal. One day, they came up to Akbar and asked, "Your Majesty, why do you always seek Birbal's advice on all matters?"

Akbar replied, "Because Birbal always has the right solutions."

The jealous courtiers said, "You can trust us too."

Akbar said, "All right. Can you find out the number of crows in Agra?"

A surprised courtier said, "How can we tell, My Lord? Crows keep flying around. They all look alike and it would be absurd to count them."

Another courtier said, "I don't think that anyone can answer this, My Lord, not even Birbal."

Akbar asked, "Birbal can you tell us?"

Birbal replied, "Yes, My Lord. There are thirty-three thousand, nine hundred and twenty-one crows in Agra."

The courtiers were surprised and asked, "How can you be so sure, Birbal?"

Birbal replied confidently, "I am sure. You can go and count the crows."

A courtier asked, "What if there are more?"

Birbal answered, "Those extra crows would be those who have come from other places to visit the crows in Agra. I have not counted those visitors."

Another courtier asked, "But what if there are less crows than you say?"

Birbal said, "Of course, there could be less crows because many of the crows of Agra would have gone to visit their friends and relatives in other places."

Akbar burst out laughing and said to the other coutiers, "Now do you see why I trust Birbal more than anyone else. He has a clever and ready answer to all questions?"

One day, Akbar asked his courtiers, "Which is the most useful weapon to guard onself with?"

One minister said, "The spear."

Another said, "The spear is too long. The sword is shorter and better."

A courtier said, "Won't a knife be better? It is small enough to be hidden in one's clothes and can be used easily and quickly."

Akbar asked Birbal, "Why are you quiet?"

Birbal said, "I don't agree with these people, Your Majesty."

Akbar said, "Then what do you believe to be the best weapon?"

Birbal said, "A weapon is not necessary. Anything that comes handy at the time of danger, is the best weapon."

No one agreed with Birbal, not even Akbar.

Abar said, "No, Birbal. I don't agree with you. You do need a weapon to fight danger. Anything cannot help."

So Birbal thought, "I must prove it."

The next day, Birbal took Akbar for a walk in the city.

They walked around for some time. Then Birbal took Akbar through a very narrow street.

Suddenly, Akbar saw an elephant rushing towards them. Akbar took out his sword, but he realised that the sword was not enough to stop an elephant.

Not knowing what to do, Akbar turned to Birbal for help.

Birbal looked around him and saw a puppy standing on one side. Birbal picked up the puppy and threw it gently towards the elephant.

The puppy landed on the trunk of the elephant.

The poor puppy got so scared that it clung on to the elephant's trunk. The sharp nails of the puppy dug into the trunk and hurt the elephant.

The elephant was beginning to get irritated. He was unable to move ahead for the puppy was blocking his view.

The lane was so narrow that the elephant could not swing its trunk to drop the puppy. The elephant started walking backwards.

As it went back, the elephant owner, who had been looking for his elephant, caught it. The puppy quickly jumped off the elephant and ran away.

Akbar heaved a sigh of relief.

Then Birbal said, "Your Majesty, your sword did not help you when the elephant was nearly on us."

"Yes, that is true Birbal," said Akbar.

"Then a harmless puppy came in handy and saved us. So it was the best weapon at that time when danger, in the form of the elephant, was closing on us," said Birbal.

Akbar took out his pearl necklace and gave it to Birbal as a reward, saying, "Thank you for saving my life."

Akbar and Birbal

Emperor Akbar said one day, "Birbal, I want to meet the ten biggest fools in our city within a month."

Birbal bowed and replied, "I won't need such a long time."

As Birbal went through the city, he saw a man on a horse carrying a bundle of sticks on his head.

Birbal rode up to him and said, "Why are you carrying the bundle of sticks on your head? Keep it on the horse's back."

"My Lord, my horse is weak. How can he carry such a heavy load of sticks on his back? So I am carrying the sticks to lessen his load," the man said.

Birbal thought, "Foolish man, this way too the load is on the poor horse only. Oh, I have got my first fool."

Birbal said to the man, "Come with me and you may not have to carry bundles of sticks on your head at all."

The man agreed. As they went along, Birbal saw a man resting with his arms spread wide open.

Birbal got off his horse and asked, "What has happened to you? Let me help you move your hands around."

But before Birbal could even touch him, the man shouted, "Don't touch my hands. I can't move my hands. I have stretched my hands according to the size of the pot that my wife wants me to buy."

"What?!!!" said Birbal, really surprised.

The man said, "See, if I move my hands then I will lose the size of the pot that my wife wants. I may get a smaller or a bigger pot, and my wife will be angry."

Birbal helped the man stand up but the man would not move his arms.

Birbal said to the man, "Put your hands down and come with me. I will get you pots of every size. Trust me, your wife will be very happy and not angry."

Then the man put his hands down and agreed to go with Birbal. Just as Birbal was about to mount his horse, a man came running and banged straight into Birbal.

Birbal shouted angrily, "What are you doing?"

The man said, "My job is to loudly call all the people to pray. I gave a call just now and wanted to see how far my voice has travelled. So I was running after my voice to see how far it would go."

Birbal said, "Come with me and you will not have to run after your voice."

He took the fools home and told his servants not to let them go anywhere. Then he went out to look for other fools. He soon saw two men fighting. Birbal rushed to stop them.

He asked them, "Why are you fighting?"

The younger man said, "This old man says that his tiger will eat my buffalo."

"But I cannot see any tiger or buffalo here," said Birbal, looking all around.

The old man said, "Look Sir, if God appears and grants us a wish each, then this man will wish for a buffalo and I for a tiger."

"And then, he will make his tiger eat my buffalo," the younger man interrupted.

Just then a voice said, "You are a fool to take these two fools seriously."

A man came and said to Birbal, "If you are not a fool, let my bones break and my blood run like this oil."

The man threw the jar of oil that he had and the oil spilled over the ground.

Then he cried, "What have I done? I have wasted my jar full of pure oil."

Birbal knew that he had found three new fools and he took them home with him.

It was a full moon night and as Birbal went out for a walk, he saw a man bent on the ground, looking for something.

Birbal asked, "What are you doing?"

"I am looking for my ring," said the man.

"Where did you drop it?" asked Birbal.

"Sir, I dropped the ring under that tree but it is so dark there. There is more moonlight here in the open, so I am looking for the ring here," said the man.

"Don't look for the ring. Come with me and I will buy you a more expensive ring," said Birbal.

The man agreed and went with him.

On the way, Birbal saw a man digging a hole. Then he looked up in the sky and started digging somewhere else. Then he dug at yet another place.

Birbal asked, "Why are you digging?"

The man said, "I hid my money here."

"Didn't you mark the place?" said Birbal.

The man said, "Of course, I did. I dug the hole under a cloud."

"Don't dig. Come with me and I will give you more money than you hid," said Birbal and took the fools home.

The next day, he took all the eight fools to the court.

"Here are the fools," said Birbal.

"There are only eight fools. I told you to get ten fools," said Akbar.

Birbal said, "First tell me if you find them to be foolish enough, then I will bring you the last two fools." Birbal told the court and Akbar about the eight fools.

Everyone had a hearty laugh and then Akbar said, "Now who are the other two fools, Birbal?"

"Both of us are fools," said Birbal.

"Me, a fool? Why?" asked Akbar.

"Yes, you are a fool for sending me to look for these fools," said Birbal.

"And why are you a fool?" asked Akbar.

"I am a fool for obeying you and going to look for these fools," said Birbal.

"You are right, Birbal. You have done very well in finding the ten fools," said Akbar laughingly.

THE MAGIC OF SUNLIGHT

One day, Emperor Akbar asked his courtiers, "Can anyone name the whitest and the brightest thing in the world?"

A courtier said, "Your Majesty, I think milk is the whitest of all things."

Another said, "I think that cotton wool is the whitest." Yet another courtier thought snow to be the whitest.

Akbar turned to Birbal and asked, "I want to know what you think is the most white and bright thing in the world?"

Birbal said, "Sunlight, Your Majesty."

The courtiers didn't agree so Akbar said, "You will have to prove this," and saying this Akbar went to his chambers to take a nap. As the day was bright and hot, Akbar ordered the curtains in his room to be drawn to make his room dark.

When Akbar woke up in the early evening, he could not see anything. He called for his servants but no one came.

Suddenly, he heard Birbal speak up, "My Lord, could you please tell me if you find the quality of cotton wool kept in the room, fine enough to be woven into a new robe for you."

Akbar replied, "But I can't see a thing. Where is the cotton wool?"

"Never mind, My Lord," replied Birbal. "Please have the glass of milk specially prepared for you."

But Akbar could not see the glass either and told Birbal to stop troubling him.

Then Birbal removed the heavy drapes from the window, and sunlight flooded the room. Akbar could now clearly see the cotton wool and the milk kept on the table right in front of him!

Birbal said, "Pardon me for troubling you. I did all this to prove that neither the cotton wool, the snow nor the milk, but the sunlight is the whitest and brightest of all the things. You could see neither of them till sunlight come into the room."

Akbar agreed, "Birbal, you have again proved yourself right."

THE DEVILISH DISGUISE

Akbar thought, "Birbal always gets the better of me. Today, I will scare him." Akbar thought of different plans to scare Birbal. Then he made up his mind to disguise himself like a devil.

He wore a devilish mask with long and sharp teeth and a horrifying face. The head had horns and was black in colour. It was quite frightening. Akbar knocked at the door of Birbal's house. The servant, who opened the door fell down with fright.

Another servant standing behind, ran to Birbal shouting, "A devil! Help us master!"

Birbal ran to see what had happened. He came to the front door and saw the servant lying on the floor. The door was open and no one was there.

As Birbal stepped out to look who was outside, the disguised Akbar suddenly appeared right in front of Birbal.

Akbar thought that looking at his disguise, Birbal would get scared.

Birbal looked at the face of the devil and then he looked down. The clothes were also like that of a devil.

Birbal looked at the devil's shoes and smiled mysteriously, much to Akbar's surprise.

Birbal was clever and knew that the devil was not real. Akbar was unhappy to see Birbal smiling.

Birbal bowed and said, "Welcome to my house, Your Majesty. I am honoured to have you here."

Akbar went inside and asked Birbal, "How did you know that it is me and not a devil?"

Birbal replied, "Your shoes, Your Majesty. They gave you away. But I am worried about one thing?"

Akbar asked, "What is the matter Birbal? You found out the truth, then why are you worried?"

Birbal said, "My Lord, I was wondering whom were you so afraid of in my house that you had to come wearing a disguise?"

Akbar was very sad that he had failed to fool or scare Birbal. On top of that, Birbal was thinking that Akbar was scared of someone in his house.

Akbar realised that no one could fool Birbal. He was too clever for everyone.

WHO IS GREATER?

One day, Emperor Akbar asked, "Who is greater, Lord Indra or me?"

A courtier replied, "Lord Indra is greater, Your Majesty."

Akbar became angry and shouted, "How dare you say that?"

Then Akbar put the same question to another courtier. Not wanting to displease the Emperor, the courtier replied, "Your Majesty, you are greater than Lord Indra."

Akbar said, "Prove it."

The poor courtier did not know what to say.

Suddenly, Birbal spoke up, "This question was put to Lord Brahma also."

"Then what happened?" asked Akbar.

Birbal replied, "Lord Brahma ordered two images to be made. One was yours and the other was that of Lord Indra. Then the two idols were weighed on God's scale."

Akbar asked, "Why?"

Birbal replied, "To see which was bigger and larger."

"And then?" asked Akbar.

Birbal explained, "Your Majesty, your idol was heavier and it bent the scale and reached the earth. But the idol of Lord Indra was light and it went up in the heavens. So Lord Indra rules heaven and you rule on the earth."

Unable to stop himself, Akbar started laughing at Birbal's wit.

Emperor Akbar asked, "Birbal, why does your Lord Krishna come running when anyone calls Him. Doesn't He have servants whom He can send? Why does He go to His people Himself?"

Birbal answered, "Because He loves all His people very much."

But Akbar was not convinced so Birbal thought of a plan. Birbal knew that Akbar loved his grandson, Khurram a lot. Birbal had a wax statue of Khurram made. He dressed up the statue with Khurram's clothes and jewels. Then he called the person who looked after Khurram.

Birbal told him, "Go to the lake with the idol. When I signal, pretend to slip and let the wax model fall into the water."

Then Birbal went to the court. In the evening, Birbal suggested Akbar to go for a stroll in the royal gardens.

Birbal walked with Akbar to the lake and signalled the man with the wax model, as planned.

That man pretended to slip and the wax model fell into the deep water of the lake. Akbar was stunned to see his dear grandson fall in the lake.

Without wasting a moment, Akbar jumped into the cold water to save Khurram from drowning.

Akbar and Birbal

But as he reached him, he realised that it was just a wax model of Khurram and not Khurram himself. He heaved a sigh of relief that Khurram was safe.

Akbar was furious and wanted to know the name of the person behind this mischief.

Birbal stepped forward and owned up the responsibility.

Akbar asked, "Why did you do this?"

Birbal replied humbly, "My Lord, why did you jump into the lake yourself to save Khurram? You have so many servants. You could have called them and let them save the Prince."

Akbar said, "Birbal, I love Khurram a lot and he is very precious to me."

Birbal said, "So, you couldn't stop yourself. That is why Lord Krishna also does not send His servants. He loves His people and they all are so precious to Him that He comes to their help Himself."

Akbar smiled and said, "As always, you are right, Birbal."

Emperor Akbar and Birbal were walking in the garden one day, when Birbal made fun of Akbar who did not like it.

Unaware that Akbar was annoyed, Birbal continued making fun of Akbar to make him laugh, because Akbar had a good sense of humour even if the joke was on him.

But that day, Akbar could not take it and he shouted, "You are so rude and insulting, Birbal. I don't like it."

Birbal's silence irritated him further.

Akbar then said, "This time you have gone too far. You have insulted me."

Upset as he was, Akbar continued shouting at Birbal, who did not say anything but just stood quietly.

When Akbar had stopped shouting, Birbal bowed before him and said, "I am sorry, my Lord. But it is not my fault."

"Then whose fault is it?" asked Akbar.

Birbal replied, "Our company influences us a lot."

Akbar asked, "You stay with me most time of the day. Do you mean you learn all these insulting things from me?"

Birbal replied politely, "Well I do spend most of the day in your company."

Then Akbar said, "Birbal, do you mean that you learn your rudeness from me too?"

Birbal did not say anything.

Akbar forgot all his anger and started laughing.

WEATHER AT ITS FINEST

One day, Akbar put yet another trying question to his courtiers.

He asked them, "When is the weather the finest?"

One courtier said, "In the summer season the weather is at its best."

Akbar said, "But it is hot in summers."

The courtier said, "It is hot but we can have cool drinks. We can also walk by the riverside and enjoy the cool evening breeze."

Another courtier spoke up, "I think monsoons are the best. It is so pleasant."

A third courtier said, "But there is water everywhere and very muddy in the monsoons. I think winters are the best."

Another courtier said, "But winters are cold, harsh and very uncomfortable."

The third courtier said, "But we can have hot drinks and sit around a fire. We have so many vegetables to eat. It is so enjoyable to eat groundnuts in winters."

Another courtier said, "No, I think springs is the most pleasant season, with flowers blooming all around."

Akbar was listening. He then turned to Birbal and said, "You have to tell me now which season is the finest?"

Birbal said, "Every weather can be the best and every weather can be the worst."

A courtier said, "Birbal's answer has no sense."

Birbal added, "I haven't finished. The most important thing is that a man should not go hungry."

Another courtier asked, "What has hunger got to do with weather?"

Birbal said, "See, if a man has eaten well and feels good, then he can enjoy all the seasons. But if he is hungry, he cannot enjoy any season."

The courtiers fell silent as Birbal said, "How can you enjoy the wonderful spring if your stomach is not full?"

Many courtiers nodded.

Birbal then explained, "If you have eaten well then you can enjoy the cool drinks of summer, the hot drinks of winter, the lovely breeze of spring and the cooling rains of monsoon."

A silence fell over the court.

Birbal continued, "Only a well fed person can think of other things and enjoy himself, no matter what the weather is like."

Akbar said, "Birbal, this is a very clever and wise reply. It has pleased me."

Akbar's wife had a brother named Hussain Khan who wanted to be a minister as he was related to the Emperor.

One day, Hussain requested his sister to help in making him a minister.

The next day, the queen pretended to be angry with Akbar.

Emperor Akbar asked, "Why are you upset, My Queen?"

She said, "I want you to make my brother a minister in place of Birbal."

Akbar replied, "Your brother is not competent enough to be a minister."

She said, "No. You have to make him a minister and that too in Birbal's place."

Akbar said, "But Birbal is doing well as a minister. How can I remove him?"

The Queen said, "Tell Birbal to do something that is not easy."

"Everything is easy for Birbal," said Akbar.

She said, "I will tell you what to do. Tomorrow when you go to the garden for a walk, tell Birbal to bring me there. I will not come and then you can tell him that he will not remain a minister."

"It won't work," said Akbar.

"It will work because I will not come no matter what happens," said the Queen.

The next day, Akbar sat in the royal garden pretending to be very upset.

He said, "My Queen is angry with me. She is not ready to meet me. Birbal, go and fetch my wife here. If you don't get her here then I will remove you from your post and appoint Hussain Khan instead."

Birbal said confidently, "She will be here in a short while."

Birbal first went to his own house and spoke with his loyal servant.

He then went to the queen and said, "I have a message from the Emperor. He is waiting for you in the palace gardens."

Just then a man came running and whispered in Birbal's ears. The queen tried to listen but all she heard was, "She is very beautiful."

Birbal said to the queen, "Now everything is changed. You need not go."

Birbal went away but the queen started feeling very jealous. Who was this beautiful lady they had been talking about? The queen had to find out.

She ran to the garden and was surprised to find Akbar alone.

Akbar asked his queen, "Why have you come? You said that you wouldn't come at all, no matter what happens."

The queen then said, "I have been tricked, My Lord, by Birbal."

Then she told everything to Akbar who said, "See, I told you that Birbal was too clever to be fooled. He fooled you."

Birbal walked in and Akbar said, "So Birbal, you have fooled my wife too."

Birbal apologised, "I am sorry, My Queen."

The queen forgave him and made up her mind that she would never again think of removing a person as clever as Birbal from his post. It was nice that Birbal remained a minister for he was a great asset to the emperor.

THE RIGHT CHOICE

After the queen had failed in making Hussain Khan a minister in the court, Hussain asked two of his loyal men to go and speak to Akbar in his favour.

They went to Akbar and said, "Your Majesty, please appoint Hussain Khan as the minister in Birbal's place."

Akbar replied, "Birbal is very clever and the most competent of all my ministers."

As the courtiers insisted, Akbar thought, "These people are adamant and might harm Birbal. I must put an end to this once and for all."

The next day in the court, Akbar said, "Hussain Khan and Birbal, come here."

Both came and bowed before Akbar and stood silently in front of him. Hussain Khan was happy because he thought that Akbar would now dismiss Birbal and appoint him instead.

But Akbar said, "This is a sealed letter that both of you will not open at all. You both have to go to Burma at once and give it to the King of Burma."

Both Birbal and Hussain Khan did not know what Akbar actually wanted but they could not refuse.

After a long and tiring journey, they reached the palace of the King of Burma. The guards on duty escorted them to the king.

When they met the king, they paid their respects to him and handed him the sealed letter from Akbar.

The king read the letter and said to his trusted minister, "See that they are put up in comfortable rooms but keep a close watch on them. They should not be able to escape."

Akbar and Birbal

As Birbal and Hussain Khan left the court, the king said to his other ministers, "Emperor Akbar wants me to hang these two men on a full moon night. I don't understand? Why were they sent here?"

A minister said, "There is something fishy in their coming here."

Another minister said, "Maybe they are important men and the Emperor did not want his people to know that they were to be killed for the fear of a rebellion."

The king said. "We must find out more about them before hanging them."

Meanwhile, Birbal began to feel uneasy. He talked to Hussain Khan and said, "I think we are in danger. Something is wrong. Will you forget that I am your enemy so that we can save ourselves?"

"Yes, Birbal. I can see the guards guarding us as if we were criminals. But what can we do? I am too scared to think. You are wise and clever. Do something."

Birbal thought and said, "I will try my best. You must repeat what I say so that both of us say the same thing."

Then a minister came to see them and said, "One of you is Birbal and the other, Hussain Khan. In his letter, Emperor Akbar has asked us to hang you both on the night of the full moon."

"What!" cried Hussain Khan with fear.

But Birbal said, "Our Emperor is great. Please do what he says."

Hussain Khan remembered to repeat, "Yes, please hang us on the full moon night as our Emperor wishes."

The king and the ministers of Burma were surprised at the way Birbal and Hussain Khan took the news of their own death. The Burmese were worried.

The king said, "Something is wrong in the way these two are prepared to die. But if we don't hang them, then Emperor Akbar will be angry with us."

A day before the full moon night, Birbal said, "Let us decide as to what we should do tomorrow when they take us for hanging. It will not help if we fear. Just let us think of a way out."

Hussain Khan was too worried to think.

Soon Birbal said, "When they take us there, I will say that they should hang me first. You should also say the same."

Next night, they were taken to the place where arrangements had been made to hang them. When Birbal saw that only one rope had been arranged for hanging them, he had an idea.

Birbal said to the Burmese King, "I should be hanged first. I gave you the letter."

Hussain Khan said, "No, I am the Emperor's relative. I should be hanged first."

They started fighting about who should be hanged first.

A minister intervened and said, "This is so strange. Why are you so eager to be hanged?"

Birbal answered, "There is a reason for this. A holy man has predicted that whoever is hanged here first, will become the King of Burma in the next birth. So I want to be the next King of Burma."

Hussain Khan said, "No! I want to be the next King of Burma."

The King of Burma got angry and said, "Only my son and no one else shall be the next King of Burma. Stop! Don't hang them. We will tell Akbar that we did not hang these two men because we are not aware of any crime committed by them. We cannot hang innocent people."

Birbal pretented to be upset and complained to the Burmese King, "Why are you not hanging us? This is most unfair."

The king ordered, "Soldiers, escort these two men safely back to their country and see that no harm comes to them."

So Birbal and Hussain Khan left for their country escorted by the royal guards from Burma. On reaching Akbar's court, they paid their respects to their Emperor.

Akbar was glad to see them back and he asked, "Did you both have a good time?"

Birbal replied, "Yes, Your Majesty."

Hussain Khan then narrated all that had happened in Burma.

Akbar said, "I knew Birbal could do it."

Hussain agreed, "Yes, Birbal is truly clever and he saved both of us."

Akbar then asked Hussain Khan, "Do you still want me to appoint you in Birbal's place?"

Hussain Khan said, "No, My Lord. Birbal is very clever and deserves his position."

Akbar and Birbal

One day Emperor Akbar saw paint peeling at many places on the palace wall.

He called his servant, Jumman and said, "Get this wall painted with lime immediately."

Jumman was not feeling well that day so he did not paint the wall. The next day, Emperor was infuriated to see that the wall had not been painted.

Akbar shouted at Jumman, "Why did you not paint the wall yesterday."

Jumman replied, "Pardon me, My Lord. I was unwell yesterday, so I could not paint the wall."

"Stop making excuses. You shall now have to eat the lime that was meant to paint the wall," said Akbar.

Poor Jumman did not know what to say. He went to get lime to eat just as Akbar had ordered him to.

On the way he ran into Birbal who asked him the reason for him being so upset. The scared Jumman narrated the entire incidence to Birbal.

Birbal then said, "You should have obeyed the Emperor. Be careful the next time. Now don't worry and do as I say."

Jumman was only too happy to obey.

Birbal asked him to get a bowl of lime mixed with some butter.

Jumman took the bowl to Akbar who asked him to eat the lime.

Jumman ate the lime mixed with butter. Akbar thought that Jumman would be sick after eating the lime but he was surprised to see a hale and hearty Jumman the next day.

Akbar thought, "Jumman is looking healthy. Why has the lime not had any effect on him? I must ask him myself."

Jumman was summoned and Akbar asked him, "Yesterday, when you went to get the lime, why did you take so long?"

"I met Birbal on the way," said Jumman.

Akbar said, "Birbal! You met Birbal. Hmmm! Bring the bowl of lime from which you ate yesterday."

Emperor Akbar then checked the bowl and was surprised to see lime mixed with butter. Akbar realised that butter had prevented any harm that lime could have caused. That is why Jumman had not become sick.

Akbar laughed and said, "Clever Birbal! He really uses his mind to save people from my punishments."

Akbar organised a contest that anyone who stands for a whole night in the cold water of River Yamuna would get a lot of money. No one was brave enough to take the test. But one poor washerman needed money for his sick child. He went to the Emperor and agreed to brave the cold water of the river.

Two men kept guard through the night to ensure that the washerman stood in the river all night.

The cold icy water reached his waist, but the washerman kept standing the whole night. Next morning, the two guards took the washerman to Akbar.

Akbar asked the two men, "You both tell me if this man really stood in the river and should he be given the prize?"

One of the two men who had watched the washerman throughout the night said, "Yes, Your Majesty, this man should be given the prize money."

But the other man did not like the washerman. He said, "My Lord, he stood in the cold water all the night, but he kept looking at the light of an earthen lamp in your palace. He took heat from it."

Akbar became angry with the washerman, saying, "You have failed the test. So you will not be given the prize."

The poor washerman came back home and told his wife that he had not been given the prize money.

Both of them were worried about their sick child, so his wife asked, "Was Lord Birbal there when the Emperor was talking to you?"

The washerman replied, "No."

The washerwoman said, "Go to Lord Birbal at once and tell him all that has happened. He will help you."

The washerman went to Birbal's house and told him all that had happened. Birbal felt pity for him; he thought of a plan to help the poor washerman.

Birbal did not go to Akbar's court for two days. Akbar really liked to have Birbal in his court because he was a clever and good minister.

On the third day, Akbar sent a courtier to call Birbal. The man came back to say that Birbal was very busy and could not come. Akbar was surprised that Birbal had refused to come.

Akbar asked, "What was he doing?"

The man replied, "He was cooking in a very strange way."

Wanting to find out for himself, Akbar went to see what was Birbal doing. What Akbar saw, made him very surprised.

Birbal was standing under a tree. On a high branch, was a pot hanging with a rope. Down below on the ground under the pot, Birbal had lit a small fire.

Birbal bowed when he saw Akbar, who asked, "What are you doing?"

Birbal said, "I am cooking, My Lord. I have put rice and pulses in that pot to prepare porridge."

Akbar said, "Have you gone mad, Birbal? The fire is down below and the pot is far up on the branch of the tree. How can the dish be cooked?"

"Why, Your Majesty?" asked Birbal.

Akbar said, "Because the fire is too far from the pot. The heat of this fire will not reach the pot high over there."

Birbal said, "But, Your Majesty, when the washerman could take the heat from an earthen lamp far away from the river, then this dish will surely get cooked."

Akbar was stunned for a moment but then he said, "Have you done this to challenge my decision making ability?"

Birbal bowed and said, "No, Your Majesty. I have done this just to ensure that the washerman gets his prize money which he truly deserves. He stood in the cold water all night. He did pass the test."

Akbar said, "Yes, Birbal. You are right. The washerman did pass the test. Thank you for opening my eyes to the truth. Call the washerman to the court."

The washerman was given the prize money who took his sick child to the doctor, and the child was soon well again. Then he went to thank Birbal, who was happy that he had helped to save a life.

THE MOST LEARNED PERSON

Emperor Akbar asked Birbal, "You have shown that there are many fools in my empire. Now I want to meet the most learned person in My empire."

Birbal said, "I will get the most learned person to meet you, My Lord."

Birbal then went to a shepherd's hut. He knew that the shepherd had a small boy. He brought the boy to his house. The boy was dirty and was wearing torn clothes. He was given a bath and dressed in clean clothes.

Birbal said to the boy, "You must remember that you have to stay quiet. Whatever happens, just don't speak."

Then Birbal took the boy to Akbar's court. Birbal bowed before Akbar and said, "Your Majesty, I have brought this child. He is the most learned person in your empire."

Akbar did not believe that a young boy could be so learned. So he decided to test his intelligence.

Akbar asked, "Where do you live? How did you become the most learned person at such a young age?"

But the boy kept quiet. Akbar asked the questions again. The boy did not answer which angered Akbar so much that he shouted, "Are you deaf or are you dumb? Why don't you answer?"

Birbal intervened, "Your Majesty, he is quiet because he is learned."

Akbar asked, "What do you mean?"

Birbal said, "This boy is learned and so he knows that silence is golden."

Akbar said, "But I am asking him questions. Why doesn't he reply?"

Birbal said, "The boy knows that he should not speak before those who are elder and wiser than him."

Akbar asked, "Is this why the boy is not talking?"

Birbal said, "Your Majesty, you are an emperor. The boy has been taught by his elders not to speak before an emperor. His learning and upbringing teaches him to obey his elders. So he is quiet as he is following what he has learnt."

Akbar nodded his head. He agreed that a learned person would show respect to his elders. So he believed that the boy was learned. Akbar was happy with the boy and gave him many gifts. Birbal then took the boy back to his parents.

THE JUSTICE OF GOD

Akbar had just decided on a case and thinking about it, he asked Birbal, "When can we see the justice of God?"

Birbal took a while to answer and then he replied, "In your empire, you, Your Majesty, are there to give justice to all. When you give a wrong punishment, then the justice of God can be seen. He makes up for the mistakes that you make."

Akbar said, "You are right. I should be careful and fair while giving justice to everyone."

DROWN IN THE RIVERS

Akbar took Birbal along when he went to see if his villagers were happy with his rule. He called a man sitting nearby and asked him, "What is your name?"

The man said, "My name is Jamuna."

Akbar said, "Your father's name?"

The man said, "Saryu."

"What is your mother's name?" asked Akbar.

"Her name is Ganga," said the man.

"Your wife's name?" asked Akbar.

The man replied, "Saraswati."

Akbar said, "Your child's name?"

The man said, "Her name is Gomti."

Birbal said, "Stop. Stop. You are naming all the rivers. Don't say the names of any more rivers or we will be swept away. Wait till I call for a boat lest we all drown in the rivers."

Birbal and all the people standing nearby burst out laughing.

THE TRULY LEARNED

Emperor Akbar asked Birbal, "We have talked so much about fools and learned men. Birbal tell me seriously, what is the real difference between fools and wise people. And Birbal, no jokes this time."

Birbal said, "It is very simple. I can easily explain the difference between a fool and a wise man."

Birbal added, "The real test of the fact whether a man is wise or foolish, comes when a person is faced with some problem in life."

Akbar said, "Explain in detail, Birbal."

Birbal then explained, "A wise man will not lose his composure when there is a problem. He will think and work out the best possible solution to tide over the problem. He will accomplish this without causing much trouble to himself or others."

Akbar asked, "And a foolish man?"

Birbal said, "In times when there is a difficulty, a foolish man would not only be unable to get rid of the problem, but could also make matters worse."

Birbal went on, "Or if the man, instead of helping, further complicates the problem then he is a fool."

Akbar said, "You are right, Birbal."

Birbal asked, "Is this the answer you expected, Your Majesty?"

Akbar said, "No. I thought that you would say that a person who has studied well would be wise, and a fool would be the one who has not received any education at all. But what you say is right. A wise man would always have control over himself and the problems, irrespective of the fact whether he has studied well or not. A wise man would use his abilities to the best and solve his problems, and not burden others with his worries."